a Capstone company — publishers for children

Raintree is an imprint of Capstone Global Library Limited, a company incorporated in England and Wales having its registered office at 264 Banbury Road, Oxford, OX2 7DY – Registered company number: 6695582

www.raintree.co.uk
myorders@raintree.co.uk

Edited by Julie Gassman
Designed by Steve Mead
Original illustrations © 2017
Illustrated by Pol Cunyat
Production by Steve Walker
Originated by Capstone Press
Printed and bound in China

ISBN 978 1 4747 2457 9
20 19 18 17 16
10 9 8 7 6 5 4 3 2 1

British Library Cataloguing in Publication Data
A full catalogue record for this book is available from the British Library.

THUD & BLUNDER

THE NOT-SO-HELPLESS PRINCESS

Written by

BLAKE HOENA

Illustrated by

POL CUNYAT

a Capstone company — publishers for children

Thud is the daughter of the town's blacksmith. She's skilled with a hammer, whether she's pounding out dings in Blunder's armour or thumping a monster. Thud is equal parts brains and brawn!
THE TOWER & FOREST
What **Blunder** lacks in size and smarts, he makes up for in foolishness. He fearlessly charges into danger, whether it's real or not. He wields his mighty broad sword and never backs down from a monster.

MAP OF THE WORLD
MOUNT MOUNTAIN
NOT-SO-DARK
DUNGEON
VILLAGE
TOWN
OPEN
FIELD
CASTLE
KIDNAPT

CHAPTER 1

SCREECH HEARD 'ROUND THE REALM

The year was Twelvity-Five A.D. The sounds of battle rang out across the land.

CLANG!

"Take that!" Blunder shouted.

CLANG!

"And that!" he shouted.

CLANG!

"And that!" he shouted again.

Blunder and Thud, two nine-year-old knights, sparred in Open Field. This grassy area was just outside of Village Town, where they lived.

Blunder swung his mighty broad sword. He struck furious blow after furious blow.

Thud raised her shield. She easily blocked strike after strike.

Clang!

"Take that!" Blunder said.

Clang!

"And that!" he said.

Clang!

"And that!" he said again.

Blunder kept attacking, furiously.

Thud kept blocking, easily. She simply ducked behind her shield and waited.

Each of Blunder's blows came a little slower than the last. And they made a little less of a clang, too.

clang.

"Take that," Blunder huffed.

clang.

"And that," he huffed.

clang.

"And – " Blunder didn't even have the breath to finish his war cry.

The tip of his sword dropped to the ground. He groaned as he struggled to raise it for another blow. His arms felt like rubber. They looked all jigglely, too.

That's when Thud struck. She lifted her hammer above her head. Then she brought it down with a **BOOM!** The ground exploded at Blunder's feet.

Blunder was thrown backwards. He landed with a **THUD**. His sword went flying from his hands. It landed on top of him with a **THUMP**.

Blunder squirmed like a worm under the weight of his mighty sword. He didn't have the strength to get out from under it. He was trapped.

Thud walked over to him. She pointed her hammer at Blunder and shouted, "Yield!"

"Never!" he replied.

Thud poked Blunder in the shoulder with her hammer.

"Ouch, that hurts!" he cried.

"Then yield," Thud said.

"Never!" Blunder replied.

Thud poked him again.

"Ouch, stop that!" he cried.

This would have continued on for hours or possibly days if a distant screech hadn't interrupted them.

It started out quiet, like the buzz of an annoying mosquito.

eeeeeeeeeeeeeeeeeeeeee

Then the sound increased to the loudness of an angry hornet.

EEEEEEEEEEEEEEEEEEEE

But it did not stop there. The screech kept growing louder and louder, until it was deafening.

EE!! EE!! EE!! EE!! EE!! EE!! EE!!

Blunder rolled over and covered his ears with his arms.

Thud fell to her knees and screamed, “Make it stop!”

The young knights wriggled on the ground in pain. The screech was so loud, it felt like the sound was stabbing their brains. Of course, that meant Thud was in a lot more pain than Blunder.

Then nothing.

Silence.

The sound suddenly stopped.

Thud and Blunder both sighed in relief. They had never heard such a deafening screech before. The noise left them both feeling a little woozy.

The pair gathered up their gear and headed back to Village Town. They hoped someone in town might know what had caused the deafening sound.

Secretly, they also hoped the cause was an Evil monster, with a capital *E*. That would give them an excuse to go adventuring.

As they neared Village Town, a rider rode out to meet them. It was one of the town's guards.

"WHOA!" he cried, skidding to a stop in front of the two young knights. "The King is asking for you two."

Thud and Blunder looked at each other, confused. "The King?!" they said at the same time.

"Yes, he's waiting for you at the town hall," the guardsman replied.

CHAPTER 2

THE ROYAL SENSES

The King lived in Castle Kidnapt, and it was rare that he visited Village Town. It was even rarer that he'd ask to see Thud and Blunder. It was so rare, in fact, that it had never happened before. Not once. Thud and Blunder were surprised the King even knew they existed.

"What do you think the King wants?" Blunder asked.

"Maybe it's about the screech we heard," Thud said. "Maybe he wants us to search out the monster that made it."

"Should we put some clean socks on before seeing him?" Blunder asked.

"No, he doesn't care about our socks," Thud said.

"But I haven't changed the left one in a week," Blunder admitted.

"We don't have time to change our socks," Thud said.

The pair rushed into Village Town's main square. In the middle of this open

area stood a large stone building. It was the town hall.

Inside, on the far side of the room, was a long table. Five men sat at it facing the pair of young knights.

One of the men had an overly large nose. He sniffed the air when Thud and Blunder entered the hall. "Do I smell a skunk?" he said.

"See, I should have changed my sock," Blunder whispered to Thud.

Another man had equally large eyes and yet another, large hands. One had a large mouth that he stuffed things into, like whole apples, an empty mug and someone's hat. The last man had bandages wrapped around his head. Large floppy ears stuck out from the bandages.

"Who are they?" Blunder asked Thud.

"They are my Royal Senses," a voice said.

The voice came from behind them.

Thud and Blunder turned to see their majesty standing in the doorway.

"Is that the King?" Blunder asked Thud.

"Who else would stand like that," Thud said.

And indeed, the King posed majestically. His arms were flexed. His crown balanced atop a head of flowing hair. His smile beamed brightly.

"Aren't we supposed to bow or something?" Blunder whisper to Thud.

"Your Highness," they said as they bowed.

The King broke from his pose and began to strut about the room.

"I have heard of your brave tales . . ." he began.

Blunder looked at Thud, confused. "Did he just say we have tails?" He tried to twist his neck around to look at his backside.

"Hush!" Thud scolded him. "Don't interrupt the King."

The King continued on, ". . . Your brave tales of heroic deeds. You battled the fire-breathing dragon up on Mount Mountain and faced the Evil Wizard in the Tower. You may be young, but you are two of the bravest knights in all the realm."

Thud and Blunder beamed. If the King said it, it had to be true.

"I need you to go on a quest for me," the King explained.

To Thud and Blunder, *quest* meant adventure. And they wanted nothing more than to go adventuring.

"Is it to find what made that loud screech?" Blunder asked.

"Um . . . no, no," the King said. "I need you to rescue my daughter, the Princess."

"Where is she?" Thud asked.

"Does a monster have her?" Blunder asked.

One of the Royal Senses stood from his seat. He was the man with the overly large eyes.

The Royal Eyes looked out one of the hall's windows. "I see her on the ramparts of Castle Kidnapt."

Thud and Blunder looked out the window, too. They could see the castle rising above the landscape in the distance. Nothing else. The castle was too far away for them to see the Princess clearly.

Thud and Blunder gave each other confused looks.

"Isn't that where you live?" Blunder asked the King.

"Well, it was," the King said. "But it has been overrun by ogres."

Things were only getting better and better for Thud and Blunder. The King was asking them to go on an adventure. And there were monsters to fight. Now if only there was a reward.

"And as a reward, I will give you something really nice," the King said.

And with the promise of . . . something really nice, Thud and Blunder prepared for their quest.

CHAPTER 3

SENSELESS ABOUT THE SENSES

"Elliot!" Blunder shouted. "Where are you?"

"Elliot!" Thud screamed. "Come here, boy!"

Moments later, they heard a **CLIP, CLAP, CLOP** coming their way. Elliot pranced up to them. Elliot was a hornless unicorn. He also served as their trusty steed on many adventures.

"Elliot, we need you to carry us to Castle Kidnapt," Thud said.

"Right away!" Thud added.

Elliot reared up and neighed,
"NEIGH! NEIGH! NEIGH!"

"Why not?" Thud asked.

Elliot bent down and sniffed Blunder's right foot.

"Did you change your sock?" Blunder asked.

"Yes," Blunder said.

Elliot neighed again.

"Well, I changed the *left* one," Blunder admitted. "It's been two weeks since I changed the right sock."

"I will pack our gear," Thud said. "While you put on clean socks, plural!"

Once Blunder's smelly business was taken care of, they were ready to go. Thud and Blunder mounted Elliot. Then off they rode.

As they were about to leave town, they saw a man waiting for them. It was one of the King's Royal Senses.

He held up an overly large hand, calling for the young knights to stop.

“I wish to offer you a hand on your quest,” the Royal Hand said. With his other large hand, he held up a gold key. “It opens the castle’s back door.”

Thud took the key from the man and asked, “Why do we need this?”

“We’ll just bash down the front door,” Blunder added.

Instead of answering, the Royal Hand turned and walked away.

The young knights thought that was odd but continued on.

They rode a little further. And another one of the Royal Senses was waiting for them along the side the road. It was the Royal Eyes. He simply said, “Look closely to see the truth.”

Then he turned and walked away.

“It’s a riddle,” Thud said.

“I hate quests that involve riddles,” Blunder said. “They are too hard to slay.”

A little further down the road, they came upon another of the King’s Royal Senses. It was Royal Mouth. As he walked up to them, he reached into his overly large mouth. He pulled out an odd-looking doll.

It looked like a rock with a face painted on it. There was also a tuft of hair glued to its back.

"This is the Princess's favorite toy," the Royal Mouth said, handing it the Thud.

"EWWWW," Thud squealed as she stuffed the toy into her bag.

"Why do we need one of the Princess's toys?" Blunder asked.

The Royal Mouth did not answer. He simply walked away.

Next, they met the man with a large nose. The Royal Nose walked all the way around them, sniffing everywhere and everything.

“I’m trying to find that skunk I smelt earlier,” he said. “I thought it had headed this way.”

Lastly, they came upon the man with overly large ears. The Royal Ears said nothing. He just put a finger to his lips to hush them. Then he handed them each a pair of earplugs.

Once the Royal Ears walked away, Blunder turned to Thud. "I think there's something the King isn't telling us," he said.

"Like what *really* made that loud screech," Thud said.

"Exactly," Blunder said. "And whatever it is, I think it's in Castle Kidnapt."

They rode all day. Castle Kidnapt loomed in the distance. But it was getting late. It would be dark soon.

"We should camp out for the night," Thud said. "To rest up before battling the ogres."

"Can we have a campfire and roast some pinecones?" Blunder asked.

As Thud unpacked their camping gear, Blunder gathered pinecones. They were one of their favorite adventuring snacks.

While sitting around the campfire, they heard the screech again. Like before, it started quiet, like a mosquito buzzing around their heads.

eeeeeeeeeeeeeeeeeeeeeeeeee

Then it grew louder, to the volume of an angry hornet.

EEEEEEEEEEEEEEEEEEEEEEEEEE

"Quick, get the earplugs!" Thud shouted.

Blunder dug through his bag and handed Thud a pair. They stuffed the earplugs into their ears just in time. The screeched turned into a deafening squeal.

EE!! EE!! EE!! EE!! EE!! EE!! EE!!

Even with the earplugs, the sound was loud. But it was not as painful as the first time they heard it.

Then it stopped.

Silence.

The quiet only lasted for a moment, though. They heard the sound of stomping feet. Something was crashing through the forest, and it was heading their way.

"We're under attack!" Blunder shouted. They both grabbed their weapons.

Suddenly, a large, greenish and warty monster burst into their campsite. It was an ogre! Thud and Blunder readied their weapons, but the ogre ignored them. It stomped through their campsite, kicking over their tent and trampling on their things.

"That's odd," Thud said. "It just ran away."

"Monsters run away from me all the time," Blunder said, puffing up his chest.

"I don't think it was running away from you," Thud said. "I think it was running away from Castle Kidnapt. Look!"

Thud pointed in the direction the ogre had come from. The monster had stomped down brush and knocked over trees. There was an ogre-shaped opening in the forest. It led straight to Castle Kidnapt.

CHAPTER 4

A SCREECH OF A GOOD TIME

Thud and Blunder packed up their gear – at least, the things that hadn't been stomped into the ground. Then they followed the path the ogre had created through the woods. It led straight to Castle Kidnapt's front door.

"It sure was in a hurry to get away," Thud said of the ogre.

"That's because it was afraid of me," Blunder said boldly.

“Ha! That’s funny,” a high-pitched voice shouted at them from above. “One of my ogres running from a scrawny knight like you.”

Thud and Blunder look up at the castle’s battlements. High above was the Princess.

“Who are you?” the Princess asked.

“I’m Thud,” Thud said. “And this is Blunder.”

“Did my father send you?” the Princess asked.

“Yes, to save you from the ogres,” Blunder added.

“Save me!” the Princess laughed. “We’ll see who needs saving.”

Then the Princess ducked behind the ramparts.

Blunder started to walk over to the front gate, but Thud stopped him.

“Come on, let’s just bash it down,” Blunder said.

“Look,” Thud whispered.

She pointed to a large vat. It sat atop the castle wall right above the front gate.

It was tilting forward, slightly, like someone was about to tip it over.

A large glob of green goo spilled from it and landed in front of the front gate.
SPLOOSH!

"We'll be slimed if we go that way," Blunder said.

"Luckily, the Royal Hand gave us this," Thud said, holding up the key to the backdoor.

They ran around the castle. At the back, there was a small wooden door. Thud slipped the key into the lock. The door opened into a dark hallway.

That's when they heard the screech again.

eeeeeeeeeeeeeeeeeeeeeeeeeee

It kept building in volume.

EEEEEEEEEEEEEEEEEEEEEEEEEE

Thud and Blunder stuffed the earplugs in their ears just as it became deafening.

EE!! EE!! EE!! EE!! EE!! EE!! EE!! EE!! EE!! EE!! EE!! EE!! EE!! EE!! EE!!

A moment later, heavy footfalls started stomping down the hall. Half a dozen large, green and warty creatures were rushing their way.

"It's a horde of ogres!" Blunder shouted.

"Prepare for battle!" Thud shouted.

Thud hefted her hammer. Blunder raised his sword. But neither of them got the chance to strike a blow. The ogres stomped right past them – and on them, too.

Thud and Blunder were left lying on the floor.

"Wow, they must really fear me," Blunder said, as he watched the ogres run away.

"Are you sure you changed both socks?" Thud asked.

"Um, maybe," Blunder replied.

The young knights stood and brushed themselves off.

"Hey! Did you let my ogres out?" the Princess shouted from down the hall.

"They ran out the door," Thud said, pointing toward the door.

"We were just saving you from them," Blunder added.

"Ha! You don't know anything," the Princess shouted. "Those ogres were my pets, given to me by the Evil Wizard."

Then Thud remembered the words of the Royal Eyes. *Look closely to see the truth.* Looking at the Princess, she'd didn't look helpless. With hands on her hips, she glared at Thud and Blunder.

"The King lied about the ogres," Thud told Blunder.

"So they weren't trying to get away from us?" Blunder asked

"No, they were trying to get away from her," Thud said.

The Princess looked mad. Her hair was standing on end. Her eyes were bulging, and her face was turning red.

She began to shout. Only it didn't sound like a shout. It sounded like the screech that they heard before.

eeeeeeeeeeeeeeeeeeeeeeeeeee

"Where are the earplugs?" Thud asked.

Blunder shrugged his shoulders, "They got lost when we got stomped by the ogres."

EEEEEEEEEEEEEEEEEEEEEEEEEEE

Thinking quickly, Thud pulled the rock doll out of Blunder's bag. She shoved it in front of the Princess.

"Dolly!" the Princess squealed mid-screech.

"Quick, let's go find the rest of the ogres while she's distracted," Thud said.

As the Princess played with her doll, Thud and Blunder ran down the hallway. It led to a large chamber.

At one end of the room was the King's throne, which was tipped over. The room was a mess. There were broken tables and chairs. Rubbish was thrown everywhere. And behind a pile of it hid the remaining ogres.

"They are afraid," Thud said.

"Of course, I am here," Blunder said proudly.

"No, they aren't afraid of you. They're afraid of the Princess," Thud explained.

And just then, the Princess shrieked from down the hall.

"It's time to introduce my ogres to Dolly," she called out.

In response, the pile of rubbish began to shake. That's because the ogres hiding behind it were shaking in fear.

"We have to save them," Thud said.

"You mean slay them?" Blunder asked.

"No, save them from the Princess," Thud said.

"So we're saving the monsters from the Princess?" Blunder asked. "Isn't that backward?"

Just then, the Princess walked into the throne room. "Oh, you're still here," she said to Thud and Blunder.

The Princess's eyes bulged and her face turned red.

"She's going to screech," Blunder said. "And we don't have the earplugs."

"Quick, give me one of your socks," Thud said.

eeeeeeeeeeeeeeeeeeeeeeeeeee

"Why?" Blunder asked as he took off one of his boots.

"Just do it, and hurry!" Thud argued.

EEEEEEEEEEEEEEEEEEEEEEEEEEE

Thud took Blunder's sock and threw at the Princess. It landed at her feet just as her screech was about to reach a deafening volume.

Then it stopped.

"EW," she said. "Did you kick a skunk with that sock?"

She plugged her nose and started to gag. The stink of the sock filled the air.

"Now's our chance," Thud said. "We need to chase the ogres out of the castle."

Blunder drew his sword and cried, "To victory!"

"And battle!" Thud shouted, hefting her hammer above her head.

They charged the ogres. The pile of rubbish exploded as the large, green and warty ogres burst from their hiding spot. Thud and Blunder chased them around the throne room, down the hallway and out the back door.

"See, they really are running from me," Blunder said.

"Only because your socks smell," Thud said.

Talk about the Tale!

1. On the road to Castle Kidnapt, Thud and Blunder meet each of the Royal Senses. Why do you think they help Thud and Blunder?
2. If you were in a battle, who would you want by your side: Thud, Blunder or the not-so-helpless Princess? Explain why.
3. At one point, Thud and Blunder wonder if the King is telling them the truth about their quest to save the Princess from the ogres. What hints did the author include to make you doubt whether the King was telling the truth?

Write about the Adventure!

1. The story ends with Thud and Blunder chasing the ogres out of Castle Kidnapt. But what happens next? Write a new ending to the story. Tell what happens when the ogres stop running from Thud and Blunder.
2. Write a story about one of the Royal Senses. What sort of quest would they go on and what type of monster would they face? How would they use their special sense to overcome obstacles?
3. The Princess was given the ogres by the Evil Wizard. Why would the wizard give her ogres as pets? Write a story about it.

GLOSSARY

battlements top part of a wall or castle; battlements often have opening spaces that soldiers can shoot through, which is awesome

guard person who keeps watch and protects a place, like a town or a person, like a tiny King

highness title of a royal person, such as a King; even short kings are called "highness"

majesty royal person, such as a King, especially one who poses majestically

quest just like an adventure, but with the purpose of seeking fame and glory

ramparts protective wall atop a castle, good for hiding behind when your enemies approach

scrawny skinny or thin, like Blunder

sparred practiced fighting; sparring is especially important if you aren't too good at it

ABOUT THE CREATORS

ABOUT the AUTHOR

Blake Hoena grew up in central Wisconsin, USA, where he wrote stories about robots conquering the moon and trolls lumbering around the woods behind his parents' house. He now lives in St. Paul, Minnesota, USA, with his wife, two kids, two dogs and a cat. Blake continues to make up stories about things like space aliens, superheroes and monsters.

ABOUT the ILLUSTRATOR

Pol Cunyat was born in 1979 in Sant Celoni, a small village near Barcelona, Spain. As a child, Pol always dreamed of being an illustrator. So he went to study illustration in Escola De Còmic Joso de Barcelona and Escola D'Art, Serra i Abella de L'Hospitalet. Now, Pol makes a living doing illustration work for various publishers and studios. Pol's dream has come true, but he will never stop dreaming.

Check out more THUD & BLUNDER Adventures!

For MORE GREAT BOOKS go to

WWW.RAINTREE.CO.UK